Amsterdam
May 2022

To Andrew and Owen

From Ms. Jeannette

Vincent and Camille

STORY RENÉ VAN BLERK
ILLUSTRATIONS WOUTER TULP

Van Gogh Museum
Amsterdam

RUBINSTEIN

Do you see that boy in the green shirt and the blue cap?
That's Camille. And the man and woman are Camille's mum
and dad.

"Bye, Mum! Bye, Dad!" Camille says. "Mister Vincent's
asked me to help him with something today."

ISBN 9789047625100

Third edition, 2019
© Rubinstein Publishing / Van Gogh Museum.
Published by Rubinstein Publishing bv / Van Gogh Museum Amsterdam
© Text: René van Blerk/Van Gogh Museum
© Illustrations: Wouter Tulp/Comic House
Translation: Laura Watkinson
Page 27: Vincent van Gogh, Portrait of Camille Roulin, 1888, Van Gogh Museum, Amsterdam (Vincent van Gogh Foundation)

"What does he want you to do?" Camille's mum asks him.

Camille doesn't know. Mister Vincent hasn't told him yet.

"Well, it'll be a surprise then," Camille's mum says.
"Off you go!" Camille gives his mum a big kiss on the cheek.

Camille sets off for Mister Vincent's house.
It's always a fun walk, because there are so many
interesting things to see on the way.

He carefully crosses the road. When he reaches
the other side, he gives his mum and dad a quick wave.

"Say hello to Mister Vincent from us!" Camille's dad
calls to him.

"Will do!" Camille shouts back. "Bye then! See you later!"

Camille hasn't gone far when he sees a steam train coming. Big grey clouds puff out of the chimney. Camille starts to run. Faster and faster. But the train is even faster than he is. Before Camille can run under the bridge, the train's already clattering and banging overhead. Camille claps his hands over his ears.

Kaboom-kaboom, kaboom-kaboom, kaboom-kaboom!

Trains are wonderful, but they certainly make a lot of noise, thinks Camille. Then the train's gone. The sound grows quieter and quieter as it disappears into the distance.

Mister Vincent lives at the end of the road, in a small yellow house with green shutters. Opposite the house is a park with a big pond.

I'll just go and have a quick look at the water, Camille thinks. *Maybe I'll even see some frogs.*

But there are no frogs to be seen. All Camille can see are some water plants and his own face. The surface of the pond is like a mirror.

Aw, that's a shame, Camille thinks. *But maybe if I wait a while…*

Then he hears a voice.

"Camille! Hey, Camille!" the voice calls.

Camille looks at the yellow house across the road. An upstairs window is open. There's a man standing at the window.
He waves. Camille waves back.

"Hello, Mister Vincent!" he calls. "I'll be right there!"

"Ah, Camille. How nice to see you," Mister Vincent says as he opens the door. "Come inside and sit down. I'll fetch you a nice cool drink."

Camille sits down and takes a good look around.

Mister Vincent is an artist. He makes paintings in all the colours of the rainbow. The whole house is full of them.

Mister Vincent gives Camille a big glass of lemonade.

"Now you just take your time and enjoy your drink," he says. "Do you mind if I paint for a while?"

"Of course not," Camille says. "What are you painting?"

"I'll show you when it's done,"
Mister Vincent replies.

Mister Vincent uses his brush to spread the paint on the canvas. He paints for a long time. Camille sits on the chair and waits. He can't see what Mister Vincent's painting. All he can see is the back of the canvas. And that's blank.

"Mister Vincent," he asks, "why is your house painted yellow?"

Mister Vincent stops painting.

"That's a very good question," he says.

"Yellow's such a beautiful colour. Yellow's the colour of the sun, of cornfields and of fresh butter.

And yellow's the colour of sunflowers too, and buttercups and leaves in the autumn."

Mister Vincent carries on painting. The brush swishes up and down over the canvas.

"So, Camille," he says, after a while. "Imagine you lived in the yellow house. What colour would you paint it?"

Camille thinks deeply about the question.

"Green!" he declares. "My house would be green. The green house! Green's the colour of grass and of leaves in spring. Green's the colour of frogs too and…"

Then he falls silent.

"No," he says. "No, my house would be blue. The blue house! Blue's the colour of the sky and of my eyes. Blue's the colour of my dad's warm coat too."

"And your cap!" Mister Vincent says.

"And my cap!" Camille agrees. Then he goes silent again. He's busy thinking.

"No," he says.
"No, the house
would be red.
The red house!
Red's the colour
of strawberries
and roses,
red's…"

"Ha, ha, ha!"
Mister Vincent
laughs. "I know
what your problem
is. You can't
choose,
can you?
You love
colour just
as much
as I do!"

Then he puts down his brush. "Finished," he says. "Thank you for being such a great help."

"Finished?" Camille asks in surprise. "But I haven't even done anything to help you yet!"

"Oh yes, you have. You did something that's very difficult indeed," Mister Vincent says. "You sat still on your chair for a long time."

"But that's not helping you, is it?" Camille says. It all seems pretty strange.

Then there's a knock at the door. It's Camille's mum and dad. They want to see if he's finished helping Mister Vincent.

"Perfect timing!" Mister Vincent says. "I've just completed my painting!"

Camille's parents laugh. "Guess what Mister Vincent's painted!" they say.

Camille thinks about it for a moment. And then he realises.

"Really?" he asks Mister Vincent.

"Really!" Mister Vincent says. Very carefully, he turns the painting around so Camille can take a look.

Camille looks at the painting. The boy in the painting looks back at him and he sees that the boy in the painting is… him! It's like looking in the mirror. Camille can see all kinds of colours: yellow, green, blue, red…

"So, young man, how do you like it?" Mister Vincent asks.

"I think it's beautiful," Camille says.

"Amazing!" Camille's dad cries.
"It's the very image of our Camille."

"And what do you think of it?" Mister Vincent asks Camille's mum.

"I think it's wonderful," she replies. "But I know one thing that's different…"

"You can't do this to a painting," she says.
And she gives Camille a cuddle and a big kiss
on the cheek.